CHEYENNE ROSE

by L. E. Williams

Illustrations by
Dan Burr

Spot Illustrations by
Catherine Huerta

MAGIC ATTIC PRESS

Published by Magic Attic Press.

Special thanks to Joe Little Coyote, Sr. and Eugene D. Little Coyote
for their help with this book. For more information about the Cheyenne culture,
check out their Eagle Wing web site at http://www.mcn.net/~coyote

Both "tipi" and "tepee" are considered correct spellings of this word. Since "tipi"
is preferred by the Native American community, we use it here.

For more information contact:
Book Editor, Magic Attic Press, 866 Spring Street,
P.O. Box 9722, Portland, ME 04104-5022

First Edition
Printed in the United States of America
1 2 3 4 5 6 7 8 9 10

Betsy Gould, Publisher
Marva Martin, Art Director
Jay Brady, Managing Editor

Edited by Susan Korman
Designed by Cindy Vacek

Library of Congress Cataloging·in·Publication Data
Williams, L.E.
Cheyenne Rose / by L.E. Williams:
illustrations by Dan Burr, spot illustrations by Catherine Huerta.--1st ed.
p. cm.-- (Magic Attic Club)
Summary: Rose travels through the mirror in the magic attic to a Cheyenne village in the
mid-1800s, where she discovers many customs of her ancestors, meets a pioneer girl, and
has her courage tested by a raging prairie fire.
ISBN 1-57513-104-8 (hardback). -- ISBN 1-57513-103-X (paperback)
(1. Time travel--Fiction. 2. Cheyenne Indians--Fiction) 3. Indians of North America--Great
Plains--Fiction I. Burr, Dan, 1951 ill. II. Huerta, Catherine, ill. III. Title. IV. Series.
PZ7.W666583Ch 1997   (Fic)--dc21   97-27256   CIP AC

As members of the
MAGIC ATTIC CLUB,
we promise to
be best friends,
share all of our adventures in the attic,
use our imaginations,
have lots of fun together,
and remember—the real magic is in us.

Alison   *Keisha*

Heather   *Megan*

Rose

Table of Contents

Cheyenne Rose
Prologue

When Alison, Heather, Keisha, and Megan find a gold key buried in the snow, they have no idea that it will change their lives forever. They discover that it belongs to Ellie Goodwin, the owner of an old Victorian house across the street from Alison's. Ellie, grateful when they return the key to her, invites the girls to play in her attic. There they find a steamer trunk filled with wonderful outfits—party dresses, a princess gown, a ballet tutu, cowgirl clothes, and many, many, more. Excited, the girls try on some of the costumes and admire their reflections in a tall gilded mirror nearby. Suddenly they are transported to a new time and place, embarking on the greatest adventure of their lives.

When they return to the present and Ellie's attic, they form the Magic Attic Club, promising to tell each other every exciting detail of their future adventures through the mirror.

Chapter One

MAC TO THE RESCUE

S o what's going on, Rose?" Megan Ryder asked. She smoothed her long strawberry-blond ponytail as she leaned back against Rose's bed.

Keisha Vance nodded. "Yes, why all this secrecy?"

"I rushed right over here when you called," Alison McCann chimed in. "Is something wrong?"

Rose Hopkins scooted her desk chair closer to her friends. She leaned forward and took a deep breath. "We're a club, right, you guys?"

"Sure, the Magic Attic Club," Heather Hardin said, looking around at her friends. "But what does that have to do with anything?"

Rose held up her hand. "Listen. I'll tell you." She pulled all her long black hair over one shoulder and twisted it as she talked. "Last night I was on the Internet with my grandfather. We were surfing around, checking out a bunch of web sites. Anyway, we found this one that was all about natural disasters."

"Like tornadoes and hurricanes?" Alison asked.

"Right. And floods," Rose answered. "Have you heard about all that flooding they're having out West?"

Megan nodded. "I saw it on the news just last night. They showed cars being washed away and houses that were under so much water that only the roofs showed."

"I heard about that, too," Heather said. "It's terrible. But what about it, Rose?"

Rose leaned back in her chair. "There's tons of damage, and hundreds of families lost their homes. There's not even enough fresh water and food for everyone."

"I know," Megan said, looking worried. "What are those poor people going to do?"

"I was wondering the same thing all night," Rose went on. "Then this morning I came up with a terrific idea." She leaned forward again, resting her elbows on her knees. "The Magic Attic Club can collect canned food and water, and send it to them!"

For a moment none of her friends said anything. Rose felt her heart thumping inside her chest. Did they think it was a terrible idea? It had seemed so perfect just a few hours before.

"But how will we get enough food to make a difference?" Keisha asked.

"We'll get the school to help," Megan suggested. "We can have a contest for which classroom brings in the most cans or something."

"Exactly!" Rose said, bouncing in her seat with excitement. "I was also thinking of getting all the other schools in town involved."

"I think it's a great idea," Heather said. "We can collect truckloads of food."

"I'm in," Alison said enthusiastically.

Megan waved her hand. "Me, too."

"It's going to be a lot of hard work," Rose warned them, repeating what her parents had said to her that morning when she'd told them of the idea. She turned to Keisha. "What about you? Do you want to join in?"

Keisha laughed and put her hands on her hips. "Do you think I'm going to let you four have all the fun and hard work without me?"

Rose clapped her hands. "You guys are the best! But we'll have to start right away. They need supplies as soon as possible."

"Let's make posters to hang up at school," Heather suggested. "If we work all day today, we should have enough for tomorrow."

"And we can make an announcement over the loudspeaker," Megan said.

"Only if the principal lets us," Keisha said.

"He will let us, won't he?" Rose asked, suddenly worried.

Rose had recently transferred from a private school to Lincoln Elementary School, where her friends were enrolled. She didn't know the principal, Mr. Roberts, as well as the others did.

"Of course he'll let us make an announcement," Keisha reassured her. "He's a good friend of my parents. I'm sure he won't say no to a project that *helps* people."

Rose breathed a sigh of relief. She didn't want anything to ruin her plans to aid the flood victims.

"Let's go to his office tomorrow morning and talk to him," Alison said.

"Maybe Keisha should go since she's the one who knows him best," Rose suggested.

"No." Alison shook her head. "We all have to go. It'll look better if there are five of us there so he knows that we're serious about this project."

"And you should be the one to tell him about it, Rose," Megan added. "It's your great idea."

"Okay," Rose agreed reluctantly. It wasn't that she was afraid to talk to grown-ups, but she was still fairly new at school. And every time she saw Mr. Roberts in the hall, he looked pretty serious—stern even.

"Then it's all settled," Alison said. "Let's meet half an hour before school starts tomorrow morning in front of the principal's office."

Everyone nodded in agreement.

Just then Little Squawk, Rose's cockatiel, flew onto her shoulder.

"*Mahpe*," he said in his funny bird voice.

Megan giggled. "What did he say?" she asked.

Rose smiled. "He said *mahpe*. It's the Cheyenne word for 'water.'"

"Oh," Megan replied, looking intrigued. Rose was Native American, and her friends were interested in

learning more about her background.

"That is so cool," Keisha said. "Has your grandfather
been teaching him Cheyenne words?"

"No. I have," Rose said, gently stroking the bird's head.

Alison's eyes opened wide. "You know Cheyenne?"

"A little," Rose replied. "My grandfather is teaching
me. And I'm teaching Little Squawk."

"Does Little Squawk know any other Cheyenne
words?" Heather asked.

"*Hese*," the bird said, as if he were answering Heather's question himself.

The girls laughed.

"What does *hese* mean?" Megan asked.

"It's Cheyenne for 'fly,'" Rose explained. "That's one of Little Squawk's favorite words."

Keisha shook her head in amazement. "That is so cool," she repeated. "Will you teach us some words, too?"

"Sure," Rose said. She put the bird back on his perch in the corner of the room. "But first let's get some posters made for tomorrow."

As the girls divided up colored markers, and Rose passed out poster paper she kept under her bed, she thought about how lucky she was to have such great friends. She had only met Keisha, Heather, Megan, and Alison a short while before, but they'd quickly become the best friends she'd ever had. And now, with their help, she was going to organize the biggest, most successful food drive ever!

Chapter

Two

THE MEETING

he next morning, Rose met her friends in front of the principal's office, just as they had planned. She held the finished posters, trying to ignore the nervous fluttering in her stomach. "I hope Mr. Roberts gives his okay for the project."

Keisha waved her hand. "How can he say no to such a great idea?"

"Right," Alison chimed in.

Rose nodded, reminding herself that her friends knew

the principal a lot better than she did. Still, that didn't make her feel any less nervous now.

A moment later, the girls stepped into the office.

"We'd like to speak with Mr. Roberts, please," Megan said to the secretary.

Mrs. Whitcomb peered through her bifocals at the appointment book on her desk. "He's only free for another five minutes, then he has some parents coming in for a meeting."

"Don't worry. We'll be really quick," Keisha promised. She flashed the white-haired woman a big smile. "Mr. Roberts is going to love what we have to say."

"Well, okay, then," Mrs. Whitcomb said, smiling back. "Why don't you go ahead in, girls," she said, waving them into the inner office.

Taking a deep breath, Rose led the way. Sitting at his desk, Mr. Roberts looked up from a pile of papers he was sorting through. For a second he stared at her blankly.

Panic bubbled in Rose's throat. Oh great, she thought, he has no clue who I am. He'll never agree to this.

But then he smiled. He stood up, holding out a hand to shake Rose's. "You're Rose Hopkins, right?" he said.

Rose nodded with relief. "Yes, I just transferred here a little while ago."

He nodded. "I remember." He greeted the others.

"Have a seat. What can I do for you girls?"

In a breathless rush, Rose explained her idea for the food drive. He nodded thoughtfully while she spoke.

"And we'll get the whole town involved," Rose ended.

"We can send announcements to all the other schools in the district," Alison said.

"I bet we can even get news coverage," Megan added. She grinned. "My dad is a journalist at a newsmagazine. I could ask him to help us get some publicity for our drive."

Rose held her breath as Mr. Roberts looked at each

girl in turn.

"The floods have certainly hit those people hard, and collecting food for them is a marvelous idea," he said thoughtfully. "But I think you need to scale your plans down a bit. Getting the whole town involved—and the news media—is pretty ambitious. Why don't you just start with our school and your immediate neighborhood, and see how it goes?"

Rose's heart sank.

"And I wouldn't recommend trying to collect truckloads of supplies," Mr. Roberts went on. "Let's try to come up with a more manageable goal—say, collecting ten boxes that you can ship there through the mail."

At this Rose felt her mouth drop open.

Heather looked surprised, too. "But there are hundreds of flood victims, Mr. Roberts," she protested.

Rose nodded in agreement. "We really want to help everyone, sir."

The principal stood up, clearly showing that the meeting was over. "I understand that, girls. But I'm telling you from experience that it's much better to start out on a

small scale. I'll approve of your food collection, as long as you keep it to our school. Okay?"

"Okay," Rose said reluctantly. She tried to hide her disappointment as she and her friends stood up. Mr. Roberts wanted them to collect just ten tiny boxes of food? That wasn't the kind of food drive that she and the others had imagined.

The girls politely thanked Mr. Roberts and left the office.

"What a bummer," Keisha said as they started toward their fifth-grade classroom.

"I know," Rose agreed glumly.

"At least we can do something," Megan said. Rose knew that her friend was trying to look at the bright side. "It's not like he said no," Megan went on, trying to convince everyone.

But Rose heaved another sigh. "He didn't exactly say 'Go for it' either."

When she got home that afternoon, Rose found her grandfather at the kitchen table with a laptop computer in front of him and papers spread out all around the table. Rose knew he was working on his hobby of translating Cheyenne tales, written in English, back into the Cheyenne language. Although it was just a hobby, he hoped to publish them someday.

He glanced up from his typing and gave her a warm smile. "Hello, Little Flower. How was school?"

Rose sat down at the table. "It was all right, but Mr. Roberts said we have to start the food collection on a small scale."

Her grandfather got up and poured them each a glass of orange juice. "That sounds wise," he said quietly.

"But Grandfather," Rose protested. She couldn't believe that he was agreeing with the principal. "We want to collect a lot of food for the flood victims. Not just a few boxes."

"Every little bit helps," her grandfather pointed out, putting the carton of juice back in the refrigerator.

"That's what Mr. Roberts said, too." Rose sighed and slid the cold glass back and forth between her hands. "But it's not what I pictured when we started all this," she explained. "How can ten boxes of food help hundreds of people?"

Her grandfather didn't say anything for a moment. "Maybe you need to be a little patient," he said gently. "Sometimes small things grow, you know."

Rose was about to protest again, but just then her grandfather changed the subject. "Would you like a lesson in Cheyenne today, Little Flower?" he asked.

Rose shook her head. Usually she loved spending time with her grandfather, hearing him talk about her family's heritage and learning how to speak Cheyenne. Today, though, she wasn't in the mood.

Rose finished her juice and went upstairs. She wasn't really in the mood for anything.

Flicking on the computer in her mother's office, she checked her E-mail. She'd sent Anna, her older sister who was away at college, a message the night before, telling her all about their ideas for the food drive.

Rose smiled at the computer screen. Anna had already written her back. Eagerly, she read the message.

Dear Rose,

I've been very busy this week studying for my midterm exams. College is so hard, but it's also lots of fun!

Your idea about collecting food is great. In fact, you inspired me to do something, too. I mentioned it to dozens of the kids in my dorm, and we're going to start our own drive. Let me know how it went with the principal this morning.

Love to you and Mom and Dad and Grandfather. I look forward to seeing all of you during our next long weekend.

Anna

Usually, Rose wrote back to Anna right away. But she couldn't bring herself to tell her older sister that Mr. Roberts hadn't been very enthusiastic about her idea. What would Anna think when she found out that her little sister and her friends were only collecting ten little boxes of food and supplies?

Finally, Rose turned off the computer and headed back to her room. She flopped onto her bed, tracing a finger along the turquoise and pink designs in her bedspread as she thought some more about the project. She still couldn't let go of the idea of a *big* food drive.

With a sigh, Rose hopped off her bed. She went over to the tall wardrobe in her room and pulled out a sweatshirt. Then she headed back downstairs to the kitchen.

"I'm going to Ellie's house for a little while," she said to her grandfather. He was still busily working at his computer.

"Okay," her grandfather said. He looked up and waved. "Just come home in time to help me with dinner."

Rose nodded and left the house. Every day she and her grandfather prepared dinner together before her parents got home from the university. Her father was a professor and her mother was a graduate student.

Outside, the brisk air stung Rose's cheeks. She

rummaged around in the garage and finally found what she was looking for—her old, red wagon. One wheel wobbled, and the paint was chipped, but it still rolled along the sidewalk.

Rose pulled it all the way to Ellie's house, screeching and clattering along behind her. If she wanted this project to be a success, even a small success, she had to start somewhere. Maybe Ellie would donate some food. Or maybe she could help Rose think of a way to talk Mr. Roberts into letting them have a bigger drive.

C h a p t e r
Three

CHEYENNE ROSE

llie greeted Rose with a big smile. "Come in, dear!" she cried.

Leaving her wagon on the front walk, Rose entered the white Victorian house.

Her neighbor shut the door against the cold autumn day. "What can I do for you this afternoon?" she asked.

Rose heard the sound of a piano coming from the living room behind the wide mahogany doors to the right. She remembered that Ellie taught music most afternoons. "Are you in the middle of a lesson?" she asked.

Ellie nodded. "As a matter of fact, I am. But if you can wait…" She checked her watch. "The lesson will be over in another ten minutes."

Rose's eyes drifted to the small silver box sitting on the table. Ellie laughed. "What a wonderful idea, Rose," she said. "You go on up to the attic, and I'll call you when I'm through. How does that sound?"

Grinning, Rose said, "That sounds great."

As Ellie went back into the living room, Rose carefully lifted the gold key out of the silver box and headed upstairs.

When she reached the attic, she pulled the tasseled cord on the hanging lamp. Even though the afternoon sun was streaming in through the windows, she liked the soft glow of the lamplight.

Rose looked around the attic, which was crowded with all sorts of interesting things—a mahogany wardrobe filled with scarves, diaries, and hats, as well as a small antique writing desk that held letters and old photographs that she and her friends loved to look through. As always, Rose's eyes were drawn to the big steamer trunk, overflowing with clothes.

She knelt in front of it and lifted the lid. Her eyes scanned the bright patterns and colors of the outfits inside. On impulse, she closed her eyes and dug both hands deep into the trunk. Velvety soft and satiny smooth material brushed her arms. Her fingers closed around small round knobs that she guessed were buttons.

Spreading her fingers wide, Rose wiggled them like worms through dirt. And then she felt it. The garment was soft, not like satin or velvet but more like a baby's sweet skin.

Gently, Rose pulled the item out of the trunk. When she saw what it was, she gasped with surprise. In her hands was an Indian dress made of soft buckskin. She peered closely at it, admiring the beadwork that someone had hand-sewn into beautiful, intricate patterns. It was just like the traditional clothing worn by Cheyenne girls and women.

Rose stood up and shook out the dress, the fringes on the sleeves and along the bottom fluttering like butterflies on a breeze. She pulled it on, then reached back into the trunk and found some moccasins that fit perfectly, along with knee-high leggings which she pulled up over her calves. She'd owned several pairs of

moccasins, but none had ever felt as comfortable as these.

Rose quickly braided her hair into two long braids that fell down her back. Rummaging through the trunk again, she found two leather thongs, which she tied at the end of each braid.

Taking a deep breath, Rose stood in front of the mirror. She smiled when she saw her reflection. "Cheyenne Rose," she whispered. To her delight, she looked exactly like her ancestors in some of the old photos and paintings that Grandfather had shown her.

Just then the walls around Rose began to blur. She closed her eyes for a second, and when she opened them, she knew she was no longer in the attic.

Chapter Four

YELLOW-HAIR GIRL

L ooking around, Rose quickly realized that she was inside a tipi. Grass mats covered with thick fur blankets were arranged along the edges of the room. On one of the blankets lay a small doll with a beaded dress. It was tucked into a toy cradle board. Leather bags hung from the walls, and in the center, a circle of stones surrounded what looked like the remains of a fire.

"Star Girl! Hurry up!" The voice was sharp but not really mean sounding. The woman just sounded impatient.

Rose hesitated. Am I Star Girl? she wondered. Uncertain, she stuck her head out of the round hole in the side of the tipi. Sure enough, an old woman beckoned to her.

"Come, Star Girl. We must finish scraping this hide."

Rose hurried out of the tipi and walked over to the woman, who was on her knees in front of a large piece of hide, the edges of which were staked to the ground.

The woman motioned to a tool made of bone. Rose picked it up. It felt strangely comfortable and familiar in her hands, as if she'd used it many times before. She knelt on the opposite side of the hide and started scraping it clean.

As she worked, she sneaked peeks around her. She counted ten other tipis of various sizes. All throughout the encampment, women were busily scraping hides or mixing things in bowls. A couple of women sat in the shade of one of the tipis, sewing. Children, younger than Rose, ran around, chasing each other. Nearby, a group of men sat mending bows and tools and talking in Cheyenne. For a moment, Rose was amazed that she could understand the language so well, but then she realized that her trip through Ellie's mirror must have had something to do with it.

Just then a boy around Rose's age approached. "Crooked Elbow," he called to the older woman. "Stick Woman wants to know if Star Girl can come help her make pemmican for the trip."

Pemmican? Rose thought she remembered her grandfather once explaining that pemmican was an Indian food made of pounded meat and melted fat.

The older woman, who had streaks of white running through her braids, sat back on her heels. "Stick Woman can't get someone else to help? I need Star Girl to help me finish getting this hide ready for tanning."

The boy shrugged.

Crooked Elbow sighed. "Go ahead then, Star Girl. Go help Stick Woman. You can help me again later."

"Thank you, Crooked Elbow," the boy said with a grin.

"Go on, get out of here, Grasshopper," Crooked Elbow said gruffly, but she was smiling.

Rose put down her tool and stood up. She followed the boy across the encampment. Suddenly he stopped and Rose almost bumped into him. He looked up and she followed his gaze. The sky was blue and clear and reached out over the prairies in all directions. Then she saw far off to the west the dark clouds rising up like smoke from a campfire.

"I wish those clouds would rain on us," Grasshopper murmured. "It's been so dry. All we get is lightning and thunder, but no wetness."

Rose looked out over the prairie. The parched grass hissed like a menacing snake as the wind blew over it. She felt an apprehensive shiver creep up her spine.

As Grasshopper continued on, Rose hurried to catch up to him. He led her over to Stick Woman, then went to join a nearby group of men and boys.

Stick Woman smiled. Rose was surprised when the woman handed her a big metal bowl. She had expected to see tools made of wood or stone or even leather. She wondered where the Indians had gotten the metal.

"Here," Stick Woman said, interrupting Rose's thoughts. "Start mixing. I've already ground up the dried buffalo meat."

Rose took the bowl. On the ground before her lay pieces of leather. Piled on top of the leather mats were several different types of dried berries. There was also a bowl filled with globs of something.

Stick Woman pointed to the bowl and said, "I have plenty of fat for many pemmican balls, so let's get to work."

Rose knelt down and started to mix the dry ingredients. Then she scooped out some of the fat and mixed it in. When everything was thoroughly mixed, she made balls around three inches in diameter and put them on a clean piece of leather to dry in the sun.

After mixing the first batch, Rose could look around while she worked. She watched some boys trying to throw a spear through a small hoop rolling across the ground. Grasshopper had joined the boys, and when his spear shot right through the tiny hoop, he whooped with joy and jumped high into the air. Rose grinned. Now she knew why he was called Grasshopper!

Then something off in the distance caught Rose's eye. A little girl sat all alone beside one of the tipis. She didn't look around at the other laughing and shouting children, and she took no notice of a woman who walked by and bent down to say something to her. The woman finally walked away, shrugging and shaking her head sadly.

Rose kept staring in amazement. The small girl had

light skin and blond hair. She obviously wasn't Cheyenne, like all of the other people Rose had seen in the Indian camp.

Stick Woman clucked her tongue when she saw Rose gazing at the child. "So sad about poor Yellow-Hair Girl."

Rose nodded, pretending she knew what Stick Woman was talking about.

"I am glad that Sun Bear adopted her into our band after he found her wandering the prairies alone," Stick Woman went on. "But Yellow-Hair Girl seems so unhappy. All day she only stares off into the distance. I wonder what happened to her family."

Rose's heart ached for the little girl, sitting so silent, so lonely. It sounded as if she'd been separated from her family. Rose wondered how long she'd been living with the Cheyenne tribe.

"May I go talk to her?" she asked Stick Woman.

Stick Woman counted the pemmican balls. "Finish this last batch and then you can go. But she won't talk to you, Star Girl. She hasn't talked to anyone or tried to learn our language."

Rose hurried through the rest of the mixing and shaping of the pemmican, then wiped her hands and ran back to the tent where she had seen the doll. Hoping it was hers to take, she grabbed it and the toy cradle board, then walked over to the little girl. As she drew closer, she slowed down so she wouldn't startle the child. But the girl didn't even look up as Rose approached.

Rose sat down beside her, holding the doll and crooning to it. She tucked it into the cradle board and pretended to comfort the doll as it cried.

Yellow-Hair Girl was now watching Rose with her wide blue eyes. Rose smiled at her, but the girl didn't smile back. Holding out the doll, Rose motioned with her head to take it.

"For you," Rose said in Cheyenne.

The girl looked at the doll. Slowly, tentatively, her hands reached out, as if she expected Rose to snatch away the gift at the last moment. Finally, she took the doll and cradle and held them gently in her arms.

Rose pointed to the doll and said, "Sweet Berry," making up a name for it. Then she pointed to herself. "Star Girl." Next she pointed to the girl. "Yellow-Hair Girl."

At this, the girl shook her head frantically. "No," she said in a whisper. "I am Sarah."

The girl had spoken in English. "Sarah," Rose repeated, smiling. "Pretty name," she said in Cheyenne.

The girl didn't smile or nod; she just stared at Rose and stroked the doll's hair. Her lips trembled and she

opened her mouth as though to say something, but nothing came out. As the girl's eyes filled with tears, so did Rose's.

"I want my daddy," the girl whispered as two shiny tears fell down her pale cheeks.

Rose nodded, letting the girl know she understood. She leaned forward and gave her a hug.

"I'll be right back," she said in Cheyenne, using hand motions at the same time to get her message across. "Wait here."

Rose stood up and looked around. She had to talk to the man named Sun Bear. Rose knew the girl would never be happy living there, no matter how kind everyone was to her. Maybe there was a way to find Sarah's father.

Rose hurried over to the group of men who were mending tools. A man stood up, and somehow she knew right away that he was Sun Bear. He was very tall and looked stern, with deep lines etched in his face and his lips settled into a thin, unsmiling line. He started walking toward another group of men.

Rose hesitated. Maybe she could just go talk to Stick Woman or Crooked Elbow. Maybe one of them could speak with Sun Bear about the girl for her.

No, she told herself firmly. If you want to help the girl, you have to talk to Sun Bear yourself. Rose started forward.

Chapter
Five

STORMY
WEATHER

S un Bear stared at Rose as she approached him.
Rose felt her legs trembling. Up close Sun Bear was
even taller than she expected. She had to squint against
the sun to look at him.

He must have sensed that she wanted to speak with
him, for he stopped walking and crossed his arms over
his chest, glaring down at her.

Rose took a deep breath to steady her nerves. She
hoped Sun Bear wouldn't say that she had no place

interfering in Cheyenne matters.

"Sun Bear," Rose began, "Yellow-Hair Girl is very sad."

Sun Bear nodded, but he said nothing.

"You have to…" Rose's words trailed off for a moment. "I mean, can you find her father?" she went on. "Yellow-Hair Girl says that she misses her father terribly."

"And how do you know this, Star Girl?" Sun Bear asked. His voice was low and growly like a bear's.

Rose thought for a moment. She couldn't tell Sun Bear that she understood English, so she said, "We used sign language," which was partly true anyway.

"Where is her father?" he demanded.

"I don't know," Rose said. "But Yellow-Hair Girl is very lonely. Please let her go home."

"She's not a captive," Sun Bear said, still not moving or smiling. "We found her wandering alone on the prairie and brought her here where she could be cared for until our next trip to the fort. We have asked everyone who passed this way to help us find her family." He paused, and Rose stayed silent as his eyes turned toward the little blond-headed girl. "I see that she is sad." He moved a fist over his heart. "I feel her loneliness. We will take her to Bent's Fort when we go tomorrow. Perhaps someone there can tell us something about her father."

Rose practically jumped for joy. "Oh, thank you, thank

you, Sun Bear. I know this will make her very happy."

She was astounded when Sun Bear's grim face broke into a smile. His even, white teeth glowed against his bronze face. Then he flicked his hand, dismissing her.

Rose flashed him one more grin, then ran back to Sarah. She squatted next to the small girl and started drawing in the dirt with her finger. Rose drew Sun Bear and Sarah on horseback on their way toward another man, trying to show the girl that the next day she would be going to the fort to search for her father.

Finally, Sarah's eyes widened with understanding. "Daddy?" she whispered.

Rose nodded. She drew several more pictures to show Sarah that she could ask some people at Bent's Fort if they could help to locate her father.

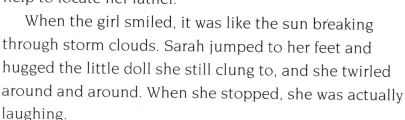

When the girl smiled, it was like the sun breaking through storm clouds. Sarah jumped to her feet and hugged the little doll she still clung to, and she twirled around and around. When she stopped, she was actually laughing.

All around the encampment, women and men and children stared. Rose realized that they'd never seen Yellow-Hair Girl smile, much less laugh. Stick Woman broke the silence with a loud hoot. Then everyone started chattering with excitement as the story of the little girl circulated around the camp. Yellow-Hair Girl was going to the fort to try to find her "daddy."

The next morning, Rose woke up when people started to stir in her tipi. Crooked Elbow was outside, piling a travois—a kind of Indian cart—with blankets, furs and boots, elk teeth, rawhide, and hair ropes. As she listened to the others talking, Rose learned that these items would be traded at Bent's Fort for steel knives and utensils, bowls, metal tools, and possibly even guns. Now Rose knew where Stick Woman had gotten the metal bowl for making pemmican—the fort.

The morning was cool, so Rose took a blanket from her tipi and wrapped it around Sarah. The little girl smiled up at her and talked on and on in English. Rose just smiled back, pretending she didn't understand Sarah's happy chatter, but inside she felt a pang. What if no one at Bent's Fort knew anything about Sarah's father? What if the girl was separated from him forever? Rose didn't want to think about that possibility.

Finally it was time for the five men and three boys to leave with Sarah. They mounted their horses, each of which pulled a travois loaded with goods to trade. Then Rose noticed that one of them was empty.

Rose beckoned Sarah over to the empty travois. Taking her hand, she helped the little girl sit on the buckskin that was stretched between the two long poles trailing behind the horse.

Sarah sat down, but she wouldn't let go of Rose's hand. Rose tried to pry her hand free. The men were ready to go and the horses were pawing the dirt, getting impatient to move.

"It's time to look for people who know Daddy," Rose said in Cheyenne. "You must let go of me."

But the girl refused.

Sun Bear dismounted and strode over. "What is the problem?" he asked.

Rose looked up apologetically. "She won't let go of me."

"I want Star Girl," Sarah said in perfect Cheyenne.

Everyone stared at the blond-haired child. So she had learned a bit of their language after all!

Sun Bear burst out laughing. "You have fooled us, little Yellow-Hair Girl," he said. Then he turned to Rose. "You will have to come with us. You will ride with the girl." With that, he turned and headed to his own mount.

Go with them? Me? Rose thought.

But before she had time to object, the travois was taken off the horse, and Rose and Sarah were hoisted onto the horse's back. They waved to everyone as they rode out of the encampment. Rose felt a surge of excitement. It would be interesting to see Bent's Fort and learn more about how the Cheyenne traded their goods for tools. Maybe she could also help Sarah to learn more about what had happened to her father.

Soon the pointed tops of the tipis were out of sight behind them. Judging from the position of the sun, Rose figured they were heading south.

The group rode in silence for a long while. Rose felt Sarah slump against her back, and she realized the girl had fallen asleep.

A few hours later, gusts of wind started to buffet them. The dark clouds that had hung threateningly in the distance the day before were now piling up one on top of the other, closer and closer. The dry grass of the prairie rustled as though an invisible hand were shaking it. Another shiver of

apprehension went through Rose. Why do I feel so uneasy? she wondered.

Just then lightning flashed off to the west. A rumble of thunder rolled across the prairie. Sarah awoke shivering, then huddled closer to Rose's back. Rose reached around and patted her on the shoulder.

"There's nothing to worry about." Rose said the words in Cheyenne, but she spoke soothingly, hoping that her tone would comfort the little girl.

As the lightning moved closer and closer, so did the booming thunder. With each clap, Sarah shivered more violently. Pretty soon, Rose was afraid the girl would shake herself right off the back of the horse.

Luckily, Sun Bear chose that moment to dismount and round the horses up into a low dip in the prairie. Rose swung her left leg over the neck of her horse and jumped to the ground. Then she reached up and helped Sarah into her arms. The little girl clung to her.

Around them, the men murmured, watching the sky and the clouds tumble closer.

Rose was startled as a spear of lightning shot through the sky. It seemed to be aimed right at them!

Sure enough, the lightning hit the ground not even a stone's throw away, with no pause between the flash of light and the following boom of thunder.

Sarah screamed in Rose's ear. Then, without warning, she tore free of Rose's embrace and raced out into the storm.

"Sarah!" Rose yelled. "Stop!" she added in Cheyenne.

Before Rose could warn her again, another terrible bolt of lightning struck nearby. Rose gasped as the parched grass immediately caught fire. Flames leaped and shimmered in a crazy dance. Rose watched in horror, unable to move, as the terrified little girl raced right toward the inferno.

Chapter

Six

THE INFERNO

For a few long seconds, Rose stood, paralyzed while several of the men and boys called out warnings to Sarah in Cheyenne. But the girl didn't stop or turn around. Instead she continued running toward the fire that was rapidly consuming the prairie.

Suddenly Sarah tripped on a clump of grass and sprawled to the ground. Her pale hair seemed to glow from the flames just beyond her. Crying hysterically, Sarah got to her feet again.

"Sarah!" Rose screamed, springing into action. As she shot forward, she was dimly aware of Sun Bear's deep bellow behind her, desperately calling for her to come back.

I have to save Sarah, Rose thought frantically. Without looking back, she ran on. Her moccasins pounded over the dry prairie grass.

The closer she got to the fire, the fiercer the heat became. It scorched her cheeks. Each breath felt as if she were inhaling liquid flames. Her lungs burned. The wall of fire grew and spread out in all directions, like a herd of wild animals circling a prey.

Finally Rose caught up to the panicked girl. She reached out with her hands, hoping to snag the back of her dress, anything to stop her headlong flight into the fire.

A flying ember landed on Rose's braid. Frantic, she swatted it out with one hand. She had to reach Sarah before it was too late.

"Stop!" she screamed in Cheyenne. "Sarah!"

The little girl stopped short and turned around, her blue eyes wide with terror. Tears streaked down her sooty cheeks.

Rose grabbed her, lifting her off her feet. The intense heat from the burning prairie nearly took her breath away. She had to squint against the smoke. Tears filled her irritated eyes, making it hard to see. Flying ashes stung like bees as they landed.

With Sarah in her arms, Rose wheeled around. She couldn't see clearly. She could only hope she was headed back toward the Cheyenne men.

When strong arms lifted her up, Rose cried out with relief. Sun Bear carried them both back to the others, his lips set in a firm line.

"That was a foolish thing to do," he said to Rose once he'd set them down.

"But I had to save her," Rose gasped. She tried to wipe the smoky tears from her eyes. "Yellow-Hair Girl was so frightened, she would have run right into the fire."

Sun Bear looked down at her sternly. Then his lips pulled into a slight smile and he nodded. "You are very brave, Star Girl."

Rose's heart swelled with pride at the compliment. She hugged Sarah closer. Sarah buried her face against Rose's shoulder, sobbing quietly.

Gently, Rose stroked the girl's hair. Bits of it had been scorched by the fire. If Sarah had gotten any closer… A shudder went through Rose. I can't think about that, she told herself. Sarah was safe now, and so was Rose.

But the wall of fire was burning closer and closer. Sun Bear motioned for everyone to mount up. They would have to run from the blaze and hope they could avoid another bolt of lightning during their flight.

Just as some of the men were mounting, a huge flash of lightning pierced the air right behind them. The tremendous boom of thunder that followed nearly deafened Rose. Then she heard shouting and yelling as big, fat raindrops fell from the black sky.

"It's rain!" Grasshopper shouted.

Rose laughed and lifted her face to the cool moisture, suddenly realizing how dry and thirsty she had been. Sarah still clutched her, but her trembling lessened as the rain fell in torrents.

More hooting and hollering sounded as the rain doused the prairie fire. They were all safe!

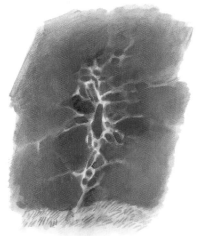

The men and boys danced around in the rain, and Rose laughed at their antics. Sarah lifted her head slowly and looked around. She didn't laugh, but she wasn't crying anymore, either.

Soon the heavy rain became a pleasant shower. Sun Bear directed everyone to mount up again. They would continue on to Bent's Fort.

Rose climbed onto her horse, and someone helped Sarah up behind her. The little girl hugged Rose's back and whispered, "Thank you."

Rose didn't say anything. She just reached back and gave her a squeeze.

Chapter Seven

BENT'S FORT

They had been riding for what seemed like hours to Rose. The rain was no more than a light misting now, but the ground was soft and muddy from the earlier downpour.

Grasshopper galloped back to them. "Bent's Fort!" he cried. "I can see it!"

Rose gripped the sides of her horse with her knees and stretched up higher. There—she could see it, too. But the fort looked different from what she'd expected. It was huge, for one thing, and its tall walls were made of adobe. Several men were standing near the entrance, as if they were guarding it. Though the settlers at the fort were probably used to traders, Rose guessed that they had to keep a close watch for trouble.

The closer the Cheyenne travelers got, the more excited and restless Sarah became. Every few minutes she peeped out from behind Rose, scarcely able to contain herself.

Rose laughed. "Hold still," she said in Cheyenne. If Sarah leaned sideways any farther, she'd fall off the horse!

The white men guarding the entrance nodded at the travelers and opened the gate for them. As they rode through, Rose looked around in wonder. Most of the buildings were of the same adobe that the tall outside walls were made of. Men and women bustled around inside, but they paused and stared at the group of Cheyenne before hurrying on their way again.

Just then, a man charged forward. "Sarah? Sarah!"

Before Rose understood what was happening, Sarah jumped off the back of the horse and landed in his arms. The man hugged her and twirled her around and around in his arms.

"Oh, my little Sarah," he kept sobbing.

Sarah's arms wrapped like ribbons around the man's neck. "Daddy, Daddy," she cried.

Daddy? This was Sarah's father? As the truth dawned on Rose, a lump filled her throat, and tears blurred her vision.

The man stopped twirling and looked up at them as though he had just become aware of the Indians. He scowled at them and backed away, still clutching his little girl in his arms. "What did you do to my Sarah?" he demanded.

Rose's heart froze. What did he mean? They had saved Sarah and brought her back safely. What did the man think?

Sun Bear dismounted and stepped forward, but the man retreated another few steps.

"Don't come any closer," Sarah's father warned.

Sun Bear stopped. Rose thought his face looked angry and sad at the same time. She wanted to cry.

"Sun Bear!" a voice shouted.

Rose looked to the left. A man with white skin approached, smiling. He spoke broken Cheyenne and used sign language to help communicate.

Rose slid off her horse and moved closer to hear better.

The newcomer listened as Sun Bear explained how they had found Sarah wandering alone on the prairie and had brought her to Bent's Fort so that she could make inquiries about her father. The man nodded, asked a few questions, then nodded again. Finally he motioned for Sarah's father to come closer.

Hesitantly, the man approached, holding Sarah's hand.

The other white man explained how Sarah had been found wandering alone. He told how Sun Bear had saved her and adopted her. Then he pointed to Rose.

"You have your daughter back because of this brave girl,"

he said.

Sarah and her father looked at her. Sarah smiled and waved.

"What do you mean?" Sarah's father demanded.

The man explained that it was Rose's idea to bring Sarah back to the fort, and told him how Rose had saved her from a prairie fire.

Then Sarah lifted the doll she had managed to hang on to since Rose had given it to her. "Daddy, Star Girl gave this to me. She's my friend."

The man hung his head, looking ashamed. When he looked up again, tears filled his eyes. "I'm so sorry," he said, stopping to let the other man translate his words into Cheyenne. "I had no idea. My brother and sister-in-law were to bring Sarah to me, but they never arrived. I don't know what happened to them. I thought Sarah was lost to me forever, just like her mother. Thank you, Sun Bear." His voice broke, and Rose felt the lump rise up in her throat again.

Sarah's father picked up the little girl, then turned to Rose. Gratitude and relief shone in his eyes. "Thank you so much for saving my daughter, Star Girl." He took a watch with a long chain out of his pocket. As he held it out to her, it gleamed in the sun that was peeking through the dark clouds. "I want you to have this," he said softly.

Rose shook her head. "Your words are enough," she said in Cheyenne. She waited for the other man to translate.

For a long moment, Sarah's father looked at her, as if he were trying to decide whether to offer something else. Finally he nodded, as if he had accepted what Rose had said. "I'll never forget what you and your people have done for my little girl," he murmured.

"Good," Rose replied in Cheyenne. Then, in perfect English, she said, "Good-bye, Sarah."

Sarah and her father stared at her in shock for a second, then Sarah giggled. In perfect Cheyenne she said, "Good-bye, Star Girl."

The two girls smiled at each other, as Sarah and her father walked away. The little girl waved at Rose over her shoulder. Rose waved back happily.

After Sarah and her father disappeared inside one of the

buildings, Rose glanced around. Sun Bear and the others were busy trading the thick buffalo furs and other items they had brought from the camp. It was time, she knew, for her to return home.

Through the entrance to the fort, she saw a perfect rainbow arched over the golden prairie. The dark clouds were rolling off to the east, leaving the sky a deep, sparkling blue.

Pride and love filled Rose's heart. She would never forget this adventure. And now, when her grandfather told her stories of the way life used to be, his words would mean so much more to her.

Slipping closer to where the trading was taking place, Rose picked up a shiny brass plate. She took it behind one of the wagons and looked into its mirrorlike surface.

The next thing she knew, she was back in Ellie's attic.

Chapter

Eight

STARTING SMALL

Rose?"

"I'll be right down, Ellie," Rose called as she slipped
off the Cheyenne dress. She folded it neatly and placed it
back in the trunk. She returned the moccasins and
leggings to the trunk as well.

She hurried downstairs
and carefully dropped the
key back in its special box
in the foyer.

"I'm in here," Ellie said.

Rose followed the sound of her voice and found Ellie in her big country-style kitchen. A kettle of water started to whistle on the stove.

"Just in time," Ellie said with a smile. "Have a seat at the table." She poured the steaming water into two delicate porcelain cups. "Now what kind of tea would you like? I have a new batch of berry teas. Let's see, I have blueberry and boysenberry and cranberry and strawberry."

"Mmm, strawberry sounds good," Rose said.

Ellie plunked a tea bag into the cup and handed it to Rose, along with a plate of sugar cookies.

After she'd settled herself at the table as well, Ellie said, "I know you came over to talk to me about something. What's going on?"

Rose fanned her tea, trying to cool it down. Then she started on the long story about the flood victims, telling Ellie about how she'd called together the Magic Attic Club members, then spoken to the principal and her grandfather about the project.

"I was surprised that Mr.

Roberts and Grandfather weren't more enthusiastic about my idea," Rose went on. She looked at Ellie hopefully. "I thought that maybe you would help me to think of a way to talk the principal into letting us hold a bigger food drive."

"Collecting food is a great cause. And I admire you for taking it on. But sometimes you have to slow things down a little and be patient."

Rose smiled. "You're right, Ellie. I guess it's okay to start out with a small food drive. Every little bit counts," she said, thinking of her adventure and about how much it meant to rescue just one little girl. "But, it's just so hard to be patient when you're excited about something."

Ellie laughed. "It certainly is," she agreed. "That's how I feel every spring when I plant new seeds in my garden. I want to see the flowers and vegetables blooming right away. But I've had to learn that gardening requires a lot of patience, too."

Rose stayed awhile longer at Ellie's, finishing up her tea. Then she stood up and said, "Thank you, Ellie, it's been nice visiting, but I'd better go home and help Grandfather with dinner."

Ellie stood, too, and patted Rose on the shoulder. "You're welcome, dear. And before you leave, I have a donation for your food collection."

Rose grinned. "How did you know I was going to ask?"

"I saw your wagon outside," Ellie said, her blue eyes twinkling. She opened up her cupboards and started to pile up boxes and cans on her counter. "I got carried away last week at one of those superstores. I don't know what I was thinking. I'll never be able to eat all this."

As the pile got bigger, Rose's eyes got wider. "You're going to donate all that?"

"Certainly," Ellie said. "That wagon you have out there is pretty big."

"But I didn't mean that *you* had to fill it," Rose said. "I was going to stop at some other houses along the way home."

Ellie waved away Rose's protest with her hand. "It makes me feel good to help those in need. Here, help me carry this out to your wagon."

Rose loaded up her arms and carried out boxes and boxes of all different shapes of pasta. Ellie carried out cartons of macaroni and cheese and jars of pickles and olives. Before long, Rose's wagon was piled high with food for the flood victims.

"Thank you so much for all this," Rose said, picking up the handle to her wagon.

"It's the least I can do," Ellie said with a smile. She waved from the front door as Rose pulled the

precariously piled wagon down the front walk.

At home, Rose left the wagon in the garage and went inside the house. Her grandfather had cleared away his paperwork. He was wearing an apron and standing in front of the stove, heating tomato soup.

"Okay, Grandfather," Rose said with a grin. "You win. I've thought about what you said, and maybe—maybe it does make sense to keep the food drive at our school small for now."

Her grandfather blinked in surprise. "What made you change your mind, Little Flower?" he asked.

Rose drew in a breath as she tried to figure the answer. "I guess it was you and Ellie," Rose finally admitted. "You both convinced me that every little bit counts. I mean, I'd still like to collect hundreds of boxes of food for the flood victims, but ten boxes is better than nothing." She smiled. "And wait till you see how much stuff Ellie's already given me!"

Grandfather folded Rose into his strong arms. "Good for you, Little Flower," he said softly. "And now, speaking of food, how would you like to help me cut up some vegetables for our salad?"

"Sure," Rose agreed. But before she reached for the bag of carrots on the counter, Rose gave him a quick hug. "I love you," she told him in Cheyenne. "Nih-mih' hodoht-dsi', nuhm-shim."

"Whoa!" Grandfather pulled away to look into Rose's eyes. "You've been studying without me, Little Flower!" he exclaimed, sounding pleased.

Rose nodded.

"You're doing so well—perhaps you don't need my help anymore," her grandfather said.

Rose shook her head firmly. "Oh, no," she told him. "I'll always need your help, Grandfather."

Diary

Dear Diary,

Well, we started off with a small food drive just like the principal suggested. But guess what? Once people in town heard about the collection, everyone wanted to help out. We wound up collecting about thirty boxes of food and supplies! And my sister, Anna, collected nine boxes at her college. Isn't that great? Grandfather was right when he told me that sometimes small things grow. It just took my being patient to understand what he meant.

Even the principal at our school, Mr. Roberts, was amazed by how successful the drive was. He came up to me in the hall at school today and told me that he was thrilled that Lincoln Elementary had made such an important contribution to the flood victims. Then he told me that he thinks I'm really brave to have started the project in the first place.

    I've been thinking a lot about what he said. And I realized that lately I have been feeling brave. It did take courage to start the food drive and talk to Mr. Roberts about it. And it took courage for me to save Sarah from getting hurt in the prairie fire. Even Sun Bear called me brave after that!

    I have to go now. I'm meeting my friends in the Magic Attic Club at Heather's house so that we can talk about our next project.

    I'll write again soon.

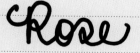

JOIN THE MAGIC ATTIC CLUB!

You can enjoy every adventure of the Magic Attic Club just by reading all the books. And there's more!

You can have a whole world of fun with the dolls, outfits, and accessories that are based on the books. And since Alison, Keisha, Heather, and Megan can wear one another's clothes, you can relive their adventures, or create new ones of your own!

To join the Magic Attic Club, just fill out this postcard and drop it in the mail, or call toll free **1-800-775-9272**. We'll send you a **free** membership kit

including a membership card, a poster, stickers, postcards, and a catalog with all four dolls.

With your first purchase of a doll, you'll also receive your own key to the attic. And it's FREE!

Yes, I want to join the Magic Attic Club!

My name is _____

My address is _____

City _____ State _____ Zip _____

Birth date _____ Parent's Signature _____

966

And send a catalog to my friend, too!

My friend's name is _____

Address _____

City _____ State _____ Zip _____

967

If someone has already used the postcard from
this book and you would like a free Magic Attic Club
catalog, just send your full name and address to:

Magic Attic Club
866 Spring Street
P.O. Box 9712
Portland, ME 04104-9954

Or call toll free
1-800-775-9272

Code: 968

MAGIC ATTIC CLUB
866 SPRING ST
PO BOX 9712
PORTLAND ME   04104-9954

|||....|..|...||||....|..||.|.|.|.|...|.|..|..|.|.||

Williams, L.E.
Cheyenne Rose

DATE DUE	BORROWER'S NAME	